T0046969

DISCOVER SERIES

AIRPLANES

AVIONES

SPANISH
Bilingual
EDITION

Avión A-7

A-7 Jet

Biplano

Bi-plane

British Harrier Jet

British Harrier Jet

F-16

F-16

Jet de Combate

Fighter Jet

Avión de Hélice Fijo-Ala

Fixed-wing Propeller Plane

Pleanador

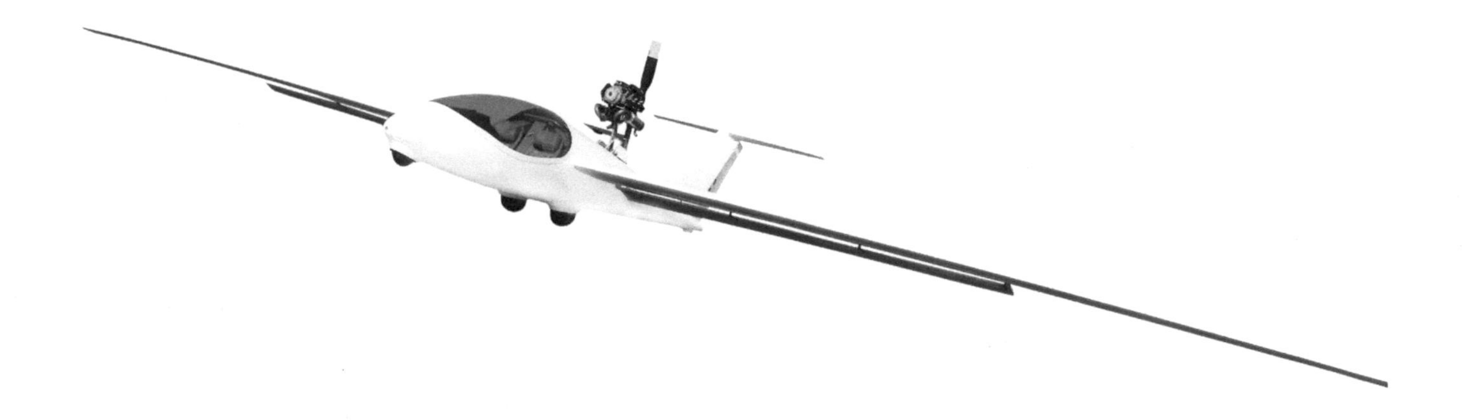

Glider

Casco de Aviador

Aviator Helmet

El Aerobús

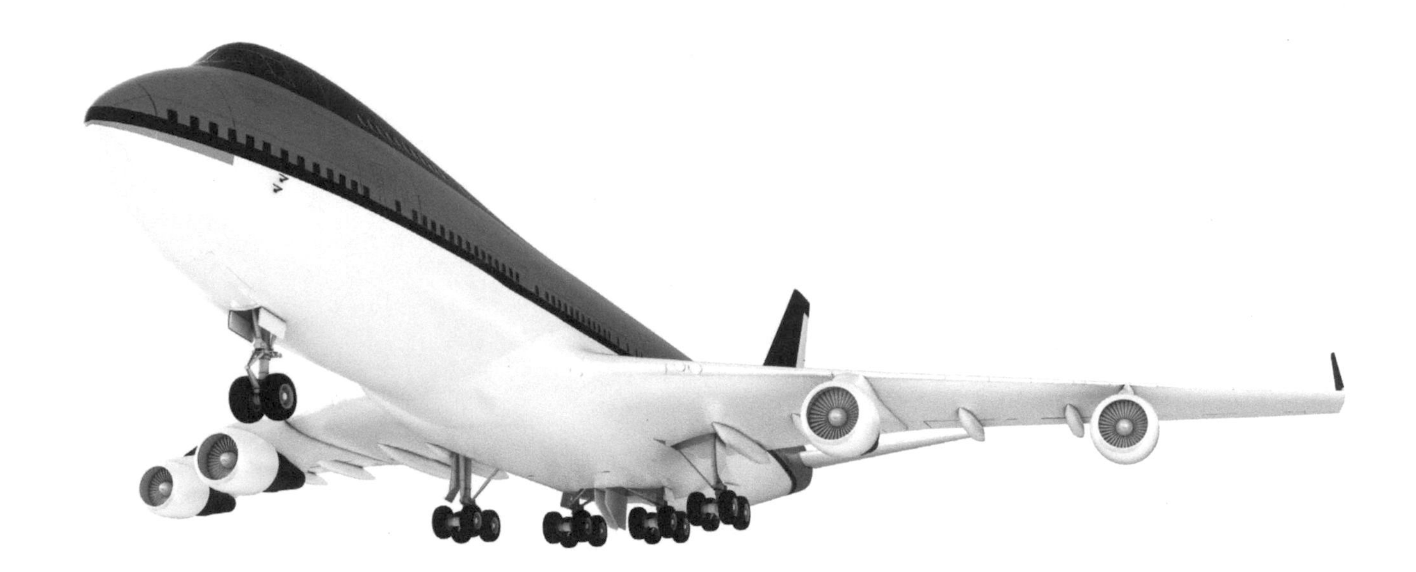

Jumbo Jet

Avión Modelo

Model Plane

La Nariz del Avión

Airplane Nose

Aeromodelismo de Edad

13
13

Old Model Aircraft

Avión de Papel

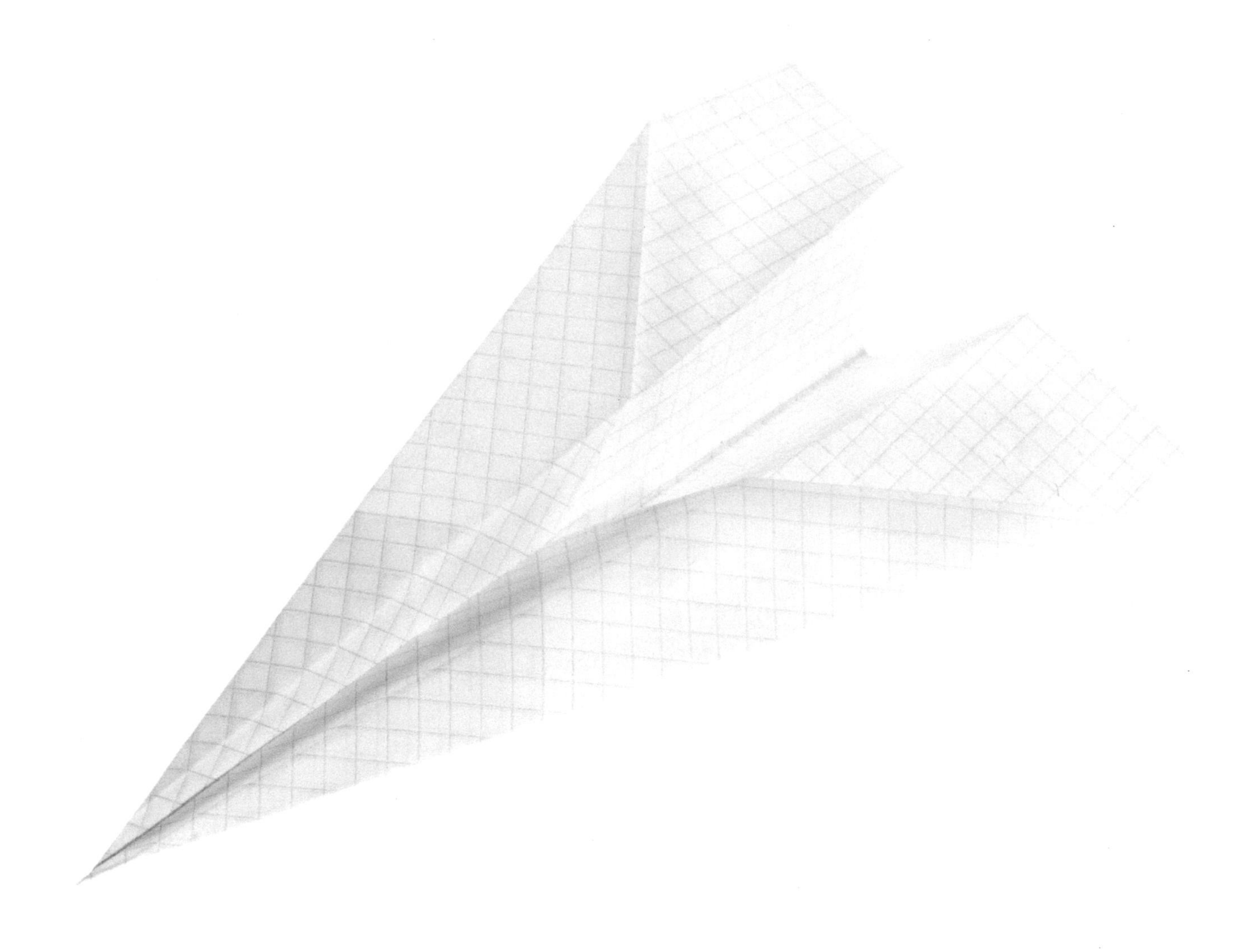

Paper Airplane

Avión de Pasajeros

Passenger Jet

Avión Privado

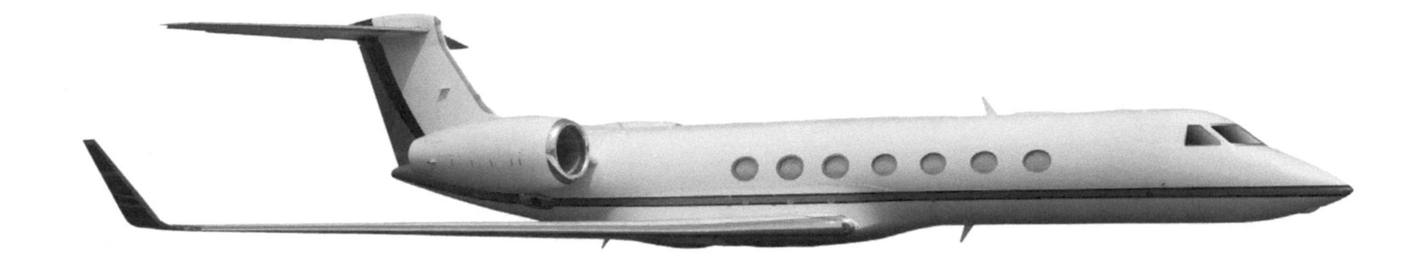

Private Jet

Avión de Hélice

Propeller Plane

Avión Ligero Fabricación Rusa

Russian-made Light Aircraft

Avión de Pasajeros Chica

Small Passenger Plane

Transbordador Espacial

Space Shuttle

Spitfire

Spitfire

Flanker SU-27

305
305

305

SU-27 Flanker

Avión Reactivo

Jet

Avión de Pasajeros Clásico

Vintage Passenger Plane

Make Sure to Check Out the Other Discover Series Books from Xist Publishing:

DISCOVER SERIES OCEAN Animals

DISCOVER SERIES
PUPPIES

DISCOVER SERIES
HORSES

DISCOVER SERIES FOSSILS

DISCOVER SERIES
BUGS

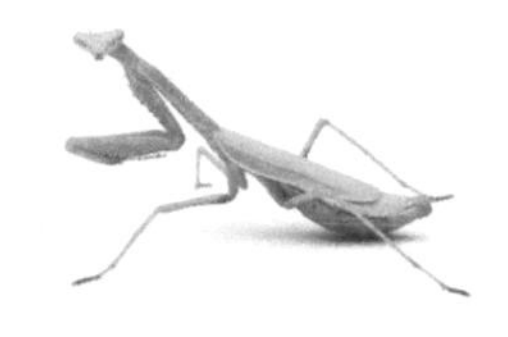

DISCOVER SERIES BABY THINGS

DISCOVER SERIES
TOOLS

DISCOVER SERIES
MILITARY Book 1

DISCOVER SERIES
TRANSPORTATION

DISCOVER SERIES
FIREFIGHTER

Published in the United States by Xist Publishing
www.xistpublishing.com
PO Box 61593 Irvine, CA 92602

© 2017 First Bilingual Edition by Xist Publishing
Spanish Translation by Victor Santana
All rights reserved
No portion of this book may be reproduced without express permission of the publisher
All images licensed from Fotolia

ISBN: 978-1-53240-084-1 EISBN 978-1-53240-128-2

xist Publishing